# AVALON HIGH
## CORONATION

# Books by
# MEG CABOT

ALL-AMERICAN GIRL

READY OR NOT: AN ALL-AMERICAN GIRL NOVEL

TEEN IDOL

AVALON HIGH

HOW TO BE POPULAR

PANTS ON FIRE

JINX

NICOLA AND THE VISCOUNT

VICTORIA AND THE ROGUE

THE BOY NEXT DOOR

BOY MEETS GIRL

EVERY BOY'S GOT ONE

SIZE 12 IS NOT FAT

SIZE 14 IS NOT FAT EITHER

BIG BONED

QUEEN OF BABBLE

QUEEN OF BABBLE IN THE BIG CITY

QUEEN OF BABBLE GETS HITCHED

## The Mediator Books:

THE MEDIATOR 1: SHADOWLAND

THE MEDIATOR 2: NINTH KEY

THE MEDIATOR 3: REUNION

THE MEDIATOR 4: DARKEST HOUR

THE MEDIATOR 5: HAUNTED

THE MEDIATOR 6: TWILIGHT

## The 1-800-Where-R-You Books:

WHEN LIGHTNING STRIKES

CODE NAME CASSANDRA

SAFE HOUSE

SANCTUARY

MISSING YOU

THE PRINCESS DIARIES

THE PRINCESS DIARIES, VOLUME II:
PRINCESS IN THE SPOTLIGHT

THE PRINCESS DIARIES, VOLUME III:
PRINCESS IN LOVE

THE PRINCESS DIARIES, VOLUME IV:
PRINCESS IN WAITING

VALENTINE PRINCESS: A PRINCESS DIARIES BOOK
(VOLUME IV AND A QUARTER)

THE PRINCESS DIARIES, VOLUME IV AND A HALF:
PROJECT PRINCESS

THE PRINCESS DIARIES, VOLUME V:
PRINCESS IN PINK

THE PRINCESS DIARIES, VOLUME VI:
PRINCESS IN TRAINING

THE PRINCESS PRESENT: A PRINCESS DIARIES BOOK
(VOLUME VI AND A HALF)

THE PRINCESS DIARIES, VOLUME VII:
PARTY PRINCESS

SWEET SIXTEEN PRINCESS: A PRINCESS DIARIES BOOK
(VOLUME VII AND A HALF)

THE PRINCESS DIARIES, VOLUME VIII:
PRINCESS ON THE BRINK

THE PRINCESS DIARIES, VOLUME IX:
PRINCESS MIA

## ILLUSTRATED BY CHESLEY MCLAREN:

PRINCESS LESSONS: A PRINCESS DIARIES BOOK

PERFECT PRINCESS: A PRINCESS DIARIES BOOK

HOLIDAY PRINCESS: A PRINCESS DIARIES BOOK

# Volume 2: Homecoming

Created and Written by
Meg Cabot

Illustrated by
Jinky Coronado

HAMBURG // LONDON // LOS ANGELES // TOKYO

HarperCollins*Publishers*

# *Avalon High: Coronation vol. 2*

Created and Written by Meg Cabot
Illustrated by Jinky Coronado

---

Lettering - Michael Paolilli
Copy Editor - Shannon Watters
Cover Design - James Lee

Editor - Katherine Schilling
Digital Imaging Manager - Chris Buford
Pre-Production Supervisor - Lucas Rivera
Art Director - Al-Insan Lashley
Production Manager - Elisabeth Brizzi
Managing Editor - Vy Nguyen
Creative Director - Anne Marie Horne
Editor-in-Chief - Rob Tokar
Publisher - Mike Kiley
President and C.O.O. - John Parker
C.E.O. and Chief Creative Officer - Stu Levy

TOKYOPOP Inc.
5900 Wilshire Blvd. Suite 2000
Los Angeles, CA 90036

E-mail: info@TOKYOPOP.com
Come visit us online at www.TOKYOPOP.com



For information address HarperCollins Children's Books, a division of HarperCollins Publishers, 1350 Avenue of the Americas, New York, NY 10019.
www.harperteen.com

Library of Congress catalog card number: 2007934417
ISBN 978-0-06-117709-5

1 2 3 4 5 6 7 8 9 10

❖

First Edition

For Benjamin

CHAPTER ONE

ONCE UPON A TIME, THERE LIVED A KING WHOSE DESTINY WAS TO LEAD HIS PEOPLE FROM THE DARK AGES AND INTO A NEW ERA OF ENLIGHTENMENT.
HA! HA! HA! HA!
HA! HA! HA!
HA!
HA!
BUT WHEN THIS KING'S LIFE WAS CUT SHORT BY FORCES OF JEALOUSY AND EVIL, HIS DESTINY WAS LEFT UNFULFILLED.

ONE SMALL BAND OF LOYAL SUPPORTERS--
THE ORDER OF THE BEAR--BELIEVED THAT
THIS KING--THE NOBLE ARTHUR--WOULD
RISE AGAIN, TO LEAD OUR WORLD FROM
THE DARKNESS AND INTO THE LIGHT.
FOR NEARLY FIFTEEN HUNDRED YEARS...
THESE BELIEVERS HAVE WAITED...
ONLY TO SEE THEIR HOPES DASHED AGAIN...
...AND AGAIN.

BUT NOW, AT LAST, THEIR UNWAVERING FAITH HAS BEEN REWARDED. FOR KING ARTHUR, CREATOR OF CAMELOT AND THE ROUND TABLE, BEARER OF THE MYTHICAL SWORD EXCALIBUR, LIVES AGAIN...
...IN THE HEART OF AN AMERICAN TEENAGER.
CONGRATS!
THANKS, ELLE.
MY BOYFRIEND, WILL WAGNER, TO BE EXACT.

JUST WHEN EVERYTHING
WAS GOING SO WELL...

I MEAN, YEAH, WHEN YOUR BOYFRIEND MAY TURN OUT TO BE THE REINCARNATION OF KING ARTHUR...
...AND THE FATE OF THE WORLD RESTS ON WHETHER HE BELIEVES THAT OR NOT...
...(AT LEAST, ACCORDING TO YOUR WORLD CIV TEACHER)...
...I GUESS IT'S HARD TO GET EXCITED ABOUT THE LITTLE THINGS...

...LIKE GETTING NOMINATED FOR HOMECOMING QUEEN...
...ESPECIALLY WHEN NOT EVERYBODY IS 100% SUPPORTIVE ABOUT IT.

BUT IT'S NOT THE NOMINATION I'M WORRIED ABOUT AS MUCH AS I AM WILL.
YOU'D THINK GETTING THROWN OUT OF HIS PARENTS' HOUSE, AND BEING FORCED TO LIVE WITH HIS GIRLFRIEND WOULD BE EVERY HIGH SCHOOL GUY'S DREAM...

BUT FOR WILL,
NOT SO MUCH.

AND IT'S NOT LIKE I DON'T HAVE MY OWN PROBLEMS.
IT'S NOT A BIG BARREL OF LAUGHS BEING THE POSSIBLE REINCARNATION OF THE LADY OF THE LAKE, YOU KNOW.
NOT THAT I BELIEVE ANY OF THAT STUFF...
I DON'T THINK.
LOOK, ALL I WANT IS FOR WILL TO BE HAPPY.
AND I KNOW THAT WHAT WILL WANTS IS FOR HIS FATHER TO ACCEPT HIM FOR WHO HE IS, SO HE CAN MOVE BACK HOME.

EVEN IF MAYBE WILL ISN'T
READY TO ADMIT THAT'S
WHAT HE WANTS.

BUT HE'LL COME AROUND. HE HAS TO.
AND RIGHT NOW, GETTING WILL BACK TOGETHER WITH HIS FAMILY IS THE ONLY WAY I CAN THINK OF TO KEEP...

...WHAT MR. MORTON'S
PREDICTING FROM COMING TRUE.

Y-YOU!

CHAPTER TWO

THUD
D-DON'T COME NEAR ME!

ELLIE, DON'T BE SCARED. LET ME HELP YOU UP. I JUST WANT TO TALK--
SLAP

HOW DID YOU KNOW WHERE I WAS? HAVE YOU BEEN FOLLOWING ME?!

WHOA, NOW.
RELAX, OKAY?

I MIGHT HAVE SEEN YOU LEAVE YOUR HOUSE--

OH MY GOD, YOU'RE STALKING ME!

NO! I TOLD YOU! I JUST WANT TO TALK--
I CAN'T BELIEVE THIS! IT'S LIKE ONE OF MY NIGHT TERRORS COME TRUE!
I'M ALONE IN THE WOODS WITH THE GUY WHO TRIED TO KILL MY BOYFRIEND.

AND NO ONE KNOWS WHERE I AM! OR EVEN THAT MARCO IS OUT OF THE HOSPITAL...

STAY AWAY FROM ME! I MEAN IT! I'LL-- I'LL SCREAM!

Hmph.

ELLIE, COME ON. DO YOU REALLY THINK I'D TRY TO DO ANYTHING TO YOU HERE, IN BROAD DAYLIGHT?
Ha ha ha!

WITH PEOPLE OUT WALKING THEIR DOGS?
WHAT DO YOU TAKE ME FOR?
COME ON, FRED...
WHINE

WELL. ALL RIGHT, THEN. WHAT *DO* YOU WANT? WHY AREN'T YOU--?
IN THE HOSPITAL?
I'VE BEEN RELEASED. I'M BETTER NOW. LOOK, ELLIE, I REALLY DO JUST WANT TO TALK.

OH, REALLY?
EVER HEARD OF CELL PHONES? THEY'RE THIS BRAND-NEW INVENTION--
SO YOU COULD HANG UP ON ME?
LOOK, ELLIE, I'M SORRY IF I SCARED YOU, BUT THIS WAS THE ONLY WAY I COULD THINK OF TO GET YOU TO LISTEN.

I KNOW HOW YOU MUST FEEL ABOUT ME--

UH, HONESTLY, I DON'T THINK YOU DO.

YOU TRIED TO KILL ME.
AND MY BOYFRIEND, YOUR BROTHER. REMEMBER?
YEAH. THAT'S WHAT I WANTED TO TALK TO YOU ABOUT.
LOOK, COULD WE GO SOMEWHERE?

JUST THE TWO OF US, TO TALK ABOUT WHAT HAPPENED THAT DAY.

DO I HAVE THE WORD "STUPID" WRITTEN ON MY FOREHEAD OR SOMETHING?

SOMEWHERE PUBLIC.
I SWEAR, I WON'T LAY A FINGER ON YOU.
TMP TMP TMP TMP

Ha ha ha!
Come on!
WHAT ABOUT HERE?
See?

HERE?

BEST I CAN DO.
SORRY IT ISN'T A THRONE, MY LADY...
I REALLY WOULDN'T JOKE ABOUT THAT STUFF IF I WERE YOU.
LOOK WHERE IT GOT YOU LAST TIME.

SORRY.
I GUESS THAT WASN'T IN THE BEST OF TASTE.
AND I WANT YOU TO KNOW...I REALLY DON'T BELIEVE IN ANY OF THAT STUFF ANYMORE.
HA HA HA!
I MEAN, ALL OF US, RELIVING SOME ANCIENT MYTH?
I REALLY MUST HAVE BEEN CRAZY EVER TO THINK ANY OF THAT COULD BE TRUE!

HA HA...
YEAH...IT DOES SOUND KIND OF NUTS WHEN YOU PUT IT THAT WAY.

Hey! Steady now!
Mommy! I wanna swing, too!

ANYWAY, THAT'S WHY THE HOSPITAL RELEASED ME BACK INTO MY PARENTS' CARE.
BECAUSE, WITH MY DOCTORS' HELP, I'VE FINALLY GOTTEN A GRIP ON REALITY...

...AND I JUST WANT TO MAKE SURE WILL HAS, TOO.

BECAUSE I KNOW THAT OLD COOT MORTON HAS PROBABLY BEEN FILLING HIS HEAD WITH ALL SORTS OF CRAZY OLD PROPHECIES--

OH, I CAN ASSURE YOU, WILL ISN'T THE KIND OF GUY WHO GOES AROUND BELIEVING IN PROPHECIES.
WELL, THAT'S GOOD.

RUSH
AND YOU BETTER MAKE SURE HE STAYS THAT WAY, ELLIE, IF YOU EVER WANT WILL AND HIS DAD TO SPEAK AGAIN.
THE ADMIRAL WON'T PUT UP WITH ANY OF THAT KIND OF STUFF.

AND YOU AND I BOTH KNOW NOW WHAT CAN COME OF BELIEVING IN SOMETHING SO RIDICULOUS AS FERVENTLY AS I ONCE DID...
Bwa HA HA HA HA!!

OH, GOD. WHAT AM I DOING HERE? SURE, HE SAYS HE'S CURED.

BUT WHAT IF HE ISN'T? MAYBE I'M THE CRAZY ONE...

TALK TO WILL, ELLIE. PLEASE.
MAKE SURE HE DOESN'T BELIEVE.
MAKE SURE HE NEVER MAKES THE MISTAKE I MADE.
IT'S THE ONLY WAY. THE ONLY WAY YOU TWO WILL EVER--
Hey!

WHAT?!
MARCO?!

HEY, BABE.
BUT HOW DID--?!
WHEN DID--?
YOU CAME TO SEE *HER* FIRST?!

DIDN'T YOU GET MY MESSAGE?
I CALLED YOU.
NO, I DIDN'T GET A MESSAGE, I, UH...
OH...
OH, MARCOOOOH...

DASH

ELLE!
WOOF!
THERE YOU ARE!
WHERE WERE YOU? I WAS WORRIED.

WILL. I'M SORRY--

NO, *I'M* SORRY.
I ACTED LIKE A JERK BEFORE. I KNOW YOU WERE JUST TRYING TO HELP.

AND IT'S NOT THAT I DON'T APPRECIATE IT. REALLY...

IT'S JUST THIS THING WITH MY DAD.
IT'S NO USE.
I KNOW HIM. AND HE'S INCAPABLE OF CHANGE.
WILL, THAT ISN'T TRUE...
PEOPLE *CAN* CHANGE.

YOUR BROTHER HAS.

CHAPTER THREE

MY BROTHER?
WHAT'S MY BROTHER GOT TO DO WITH ANY OF THIS?
I JUST SAW HIM OVER AT THE ARBORETUM.
WILL, HE'S OUT OF THE HOSPITAL. AND HE SEEMS BETTER. MUCH BETTER...
TURN

HE'S REALLY WORRIED ABOUT YOU, IN FACT, WILL.

THAT'S IMPOSSIBLE.
ELLE, WHATEVER HE SAID TO YOU-- WHATEVER HE TOLD YOU, IT WAS AN ACT.

NO, WILL. REALLY!

I THOUGHT SO, TOO...AT FIRST. BUT NOW...I'M NOT SO SURE.
I THINK HE REALLY MIGHT HAVE CHANGED. HE SEEMED REALLY CONCERNED ABOUT YOU.

HE WANTS TO TRY TO MAKE THINGS RIGHT--

ELLE, DO I HAVE TO REMIND YOU THAT JUST A COUPLE OF MONTHS AGO THAT GUY TRIED TO KILL US BOTH?!
JUMP
YOU MIGHT BE WILLING TO FORGIVE AND FORGET THAT...
...BUT I'M NOT.

Meow?
SLUMP

GREAT. NOW WILL AND I ARE HAVING OUR FIRST REAL FIGHT... AND IT'S NOT ONE I HAVE ANY HOPE OF WINNING.
Huff!
Huff!
Nngh...

ELLE? ELLE, YOU'RE DREAMING. WAKE UP.

ELLE! ELLE! SHHH, YOU'LL WAKE YOUR PARENTS.

JOLT
NO!
ELLE, IT'S ALL RIGHT. IT WAS JUST A DREAM.
OH, WILL. IT WAS SO HORRIBLE!

IT'S OKAY NOW, I'M HERE.
WHAT WAS IT THIS TIME? DO YOU REMEMBER WHAT HAPPENED?

HOW CAN I TELL HIM?

HOW CAN I TELL HIM THAT HE WAS RIGHT-- HE HAD TO HAVE BEEN RIGHT--ABOUT HIS BROTHER ALL ALONG?

IT'S JUST A DREAM.
NO... NOT A DREAM. A NIGHTMARE.

I...
I DON'T
KNOW.
POOR ELLE.
WHAT CAN I DO TO
MAKE IT BETTER?
Have dinner
with your
parents?

WHAT?!

HAVE DINNER WITH YOUR PARENTS.
PLEASE, WILL? YOUR MOTHER MISSES YOU SO MUCH.

I CAN'T BELIEVE THIS. WAS THIS A SETUP?!

NO!
WILL. *NO.*
BUT COME ON. YOUR MOM--

AND NOW MARCO IS HOME. YOU EXPECT ME TO HAVE DINNER WITH MARCO, TOO?
NO! JUST YOUR PARENTS.
PLEASE?
FOR ME?

FINE! IF IT MEANS THAT MUCH TO YOU.
BUT ONLY IF YOUR PARENTS COME, TOO...AND IT'S AT SOME NEUTRAL LOCATION, LIKE A RESTAURANT, SO MY FATHER CAN'T MAKE A SCENE.
BUT DON'T EXPECT TOO MUCH FROM IT, ELLE. I'M WARNING YOU... MY DAD IS EVERY BIT AS STUBBORN AS I AM.
OH, *WILL!*

TWEET
TWEET
THE NEXT DAY AT SCHOOL...
Yeah, so then...
Oh?
RRIP
RRRIP
JENNIFER

RRRIP
WHAT'S GOING ON, YOU GUYS? WHY ARE YOU...?
OH.
YEAH. THEY'RE ALL LIKE THAT.

SOME TROLL MUST'VE GONE THROUGH EARLY THIS MORNING AND TRASHED EVERY SINGLE ONE OF OUR POSTERS.
VOTE
ONE GUESS AS TO WHO THAT TROLL MIGHT HAVE BEEN.
GIRLS SCARE ME SOMETIMES.

WHAT ARE WE GOING TO DO?

EASY. MAKE *NEW* POSTERS!

All right!
SLAP
Let's do it!

NO. YOU GUYS.
LET'S JUST FORGET ABOUT IT.
FLUTTER

NO WAY.

WILL'S RIGHT. NO WAY ARE WE GOING TO FORGET ABOUT IT.
WE'LL MEET IN THE ART ROOM AT LUNCH AND JUST MAKE NEW ONES. RIGHT AFTER I COMPLAIN TO THE VICE-PRINCIPAL--
JENNIFER, NO!

IT'S *MY* PROBLEM--LET *ME* HANDLE IT.
ARE YOU SURE?
OH, I'M SURE.
NOW *I'M* SCARED.
SEE WHAT I MEAN?

RESTROOM

OH. IT'S JUST *YOU.*
I THOUGHT IT WAS A TEACHER.

WHAT ARE YOU DOING, MISSING THE BELL?
I THOUGHT YOU WERE ONE OF THOSE STRAIGHT-A, NEVER-SKIPS-A CLASS TYPES?

MY FRIENDS WORKED REALLY HARD ON THOSE POSTERS, MORGAN.

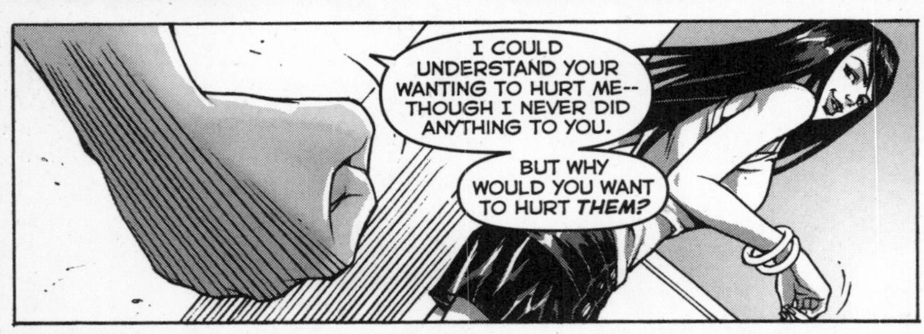
I COULD UNDERSTAND YOUR WANTING TO HURT ME-- THOUGH I NEVER DID ANYTHING TO YOU.
BUT WHY WOULD YOU WANT TO HURT *THEM?*

OH, RIGHT.
SO THAT *WASN'T* YOU I SAW MAKING OUT WITH MY BOYFRIEND IN THE PARK LAST NIGHT?

MARCO AND I WERE JUST TALKING!
DIDN'T HE TELL YOU THAT?
SMIRK
WELL, LET'S FACE IT, ELLIE...
HOMECOMING QUEEN

IT'S NOT LIKE YOU DON'T HAVE A HISTORY OF STEALING OTHER PEOPLE'S BOYFRIENDS.
YOU KNOW PERFECTLY WELL I DIDN'T STEAL WILL FROM ANYONE!

RIGHT.
JUST LIKE YOUR GOOD FRIEND JENNIFER WASN'T CATTING AROUND WITH HER BOYFRIEND'S BEST FRIEND BEHIND HIS BACK.
YOU'VE BEEN SEEING MARCO BEHIND WILL'S BACK, ALL RIGHT.

OR AT LEAST, THAT'S WHAT I PLAN ON TELLING HIM...

...UNLESS YOU DROP OUT OF THE HOMECOMING QUEEN RACE.

CHAPTER FOUR

JENNIFER
THAT'S WHAT I PLAN ON TELLING HIM...
...UNLESS YOU DROP OUT OF THE HOMECOMING QUEEN RACE.

YOU HAVE *GOT* TO BE KIDDING ME.
pfft!
HOW WELL DO YOU THINK WILL IS GOING TO TAKE THE NEWS THAT HIS NEW GIRLFRIEND IS SEEING HIS HALF BROTHER BEHIND HIS BACK?
ESPECIALLY CONSIDERING WHAT HE FOUND OUT ABOUT HIS LAST GIRLFRIEND AND HIS BEST FRIEND JUST A FEW MONTHS AGO?

WHAT IS THE MATTER WITH YOU?
HOW CAN YOU BE SO...
SO...!
HOT?
CLENCH
EVIL!

WORD OF ADVICE, ELLIE.
YOU MAY BE A TRACK STAR AND WELL-LIKED ENOUGH TO HAVE BEEN NOMINATED FOR HOMECOMING QUEEN.

YOU MAY BE JENNIFER GOLD'S NEW BEST FRIEND, AND YOU MAY EVEN BE DATING THE QUARTERBACK.

BUT YOU'RE STILL THE NEW GIRL AS FAR AS *I'M* CONCERNED. AND YOU'D BETTER DO WHAT I SAY...
...OR YOU'LL REGRET IT.

TMP
TMP
TMP

BRRRRRING

ELLIE, COULD YOU STAY A MINUTE AFTER CLASS?

SURE, MR. M...

ELLIE, WHAT'S ALL THIS I'VE HEARD ABOUT YOU PLANNING A DINNER WITH WILL'S PARENTS?

OH.
YOU HEARD ABOUT THAT? I--
SLAM

DON'T YOU KNOW THAT THIS IS THE ABSOLUTE WORST THING YOU COULD BE DOING RIGHT NOW, WITH THE HUNTER'S MOON DUE TO RISE DAY AFTER TOMORROW?!

THE ADMIRAL ISN'T A BELIEVER, AND THE LAST THING WILL NEEDS...

...IS MORE INFLUENCE FROM NON-BELIEVERS.

WELL, IF KEEPING SONS FROM DINING WITH THEIR FATHERS IS SOMETHING THE ORDER OF THE BEAR SUPPORTS, THEN MAYBE YOU SHOULD COUNT *ME* AS A NON-BELIEVER AS WELL.
ELLIE! WHAT'S WRONG WITH YOU?!

AND BY THE WAY, DO YOU KNOW THAT MARCO IS BACK HOME, LIVING WITH HIS PARENTS?

W-WHAT? NO. NO, I DIDN'T....
WELL, IT'S TRUE. AND HE'S DOING MUCH BETTER. HE NO LONGER BELIEVES THAT HE'S THE REINCARNATION OF MORDRED.

APPARENTLY, HE NO LONGER POSES A THREAT TO ANYONE.

BUT EVEN AS I SAID IT, I KNEW IT WASN'T TRUE. MY NIGHTMARES TOLD ME OTHERWISE.

BUT AFTER ALL, THEY'RE ONLY NIGHTMARES. THEY DON'T **MEAN** ANYTHING.

DO THEY?

IT SIMPLY CAN'T BE TRUE.
THE BOY MUST BE LYING.
THE DARK SIDE'S GRIP ON MORDRED IS SIMPLY TOO STRONG TO HAVE BEEN SO EASILY OVERCOME IN SUCH A SHORT TIME.

MR. MORTON! COME ON! WE LIVE IN THE REAL WORLD!

YOU NEED TO GET OVER THIS KING ARTHUR BUSINESS. WILL IS ***NOT*** A REINCARNATED KING, HE'S JUST A TEENAGE BOY WITH FAMILY PROBLEMS!
AND YOU'RE ***NOT*** HELPING THOSE PROBLEMS WITH ALL THIS STUFF ABOUT THE MERLIN PROPHECY.

WHY CAN'T YOU JUST LET WILL ENJOY HIS LAST YEAR IN HIGH SCHOOL?

BRRRRING

TURN

HOW HAVE YOU BEEN SLEEPING LATELY, ELLIE?

HOW DID--?
OH. WILL TOLD YOU.

WILL DID TELL ME... BUT HE DIDN'T HAVE TO.
LET ME ASK YOU SOMETHING, ELLIE--IF YOU'RE SO TRULY CONVINCED THAT MARCO DOESN'T MEAN WILL ANY HARM, WHY ARE YOU STILL SO AFRAID OF HIM THAT YOU DREAM OF HIM EVERY NIGHT?

I NEVER TOLD--

YOU NEVER TOLD WILL YOUR DREAMS WERE ABOUT MARCO? YOU DIDN'T HAVE TO. I KNOW.

YOU KNOW FULL WELL...

...THAT WILL ISN'T MERELY A TEENAGE BOY WITH FAMILY PROBLEMS.
YOUR NIGHTMARES ARE DIRECTLY RELATED TO THE MERLIN PROPHECY, AND THEY'RE TELLING YOU THE SAME THING MINE ARE TELLING ME.
TIME IS RUNNING OUT, NOT JUST FOR WILL...BUT FOR THE WORLD AS WELL.

BECAUSE IF WILL DOESN'T EMBRACE HIS TRUE IDENTITY BY THE NIGHT OF THE HUNTER'S MOON...

...EVERYTHING WILL BE LOST!

DOOOOOM
AND THAT INCLUDES ANY HOPE I MIGHT HARBOR OF A HAPPY FUTURE WITH THE GUY OF MY DREAMS.
AND I DO MEAN MY **DREAMS**, AND **NOT** MY NIGHT-MARES.

SO, ELLIE.
LET'S DO A BIT LESS WORRYING ABOUT HOMECOMING QUEEN AND FAMILY DINNERS, AND A BIT MORE WORRYING ABOUT THE FATE OF THE PLANET. SHALL WE?
DASH

WAIT... WHERE IS EVERYBODY?

GAB
GAB
GAB
GAB
GAB
GAB
GAB
GAB
GAB
COULD MORGAN HAVE TOLD THEM ALREADY?
TMP
TMP
TMP

BUT...THEY'D NEVER HAVE BELIEVED HER.
ART RM.
ESPECIALLY NOT... NOT WILL...
AAAH!

CHAPTER FIVE

GASP!

SURPRISE!
HOME
sniffle

OH... YOU GUYS...

YOU LIKE?
WE THINK THEY'RE EVEN BETTER THAN BEFORE.

MINE'S SUPPOSED TO BE *IMPRESSIONISTIC.*
VOTE 4
THE IMPORTANT THING IS THAT YOU TRIED.

AND ABOUT YOUR DRESS--YOU TOOK OFF SO FAST THE OTHER NIGHT, AFTER WE SAW MRS. WAGNER, WITHOUT EVEN TRYING ANYTHING ON.

I WANT YOU TO KNOW, I PICKED ONE OUT FOR YOU.

WHAT? JENNIFER, NO--

MY TREAT.
AND *MY* SURPRISE.

UM...
SHOULD I BE AFRAID?

*VERY* AFRAID.
GRIN

RRRRRRING
Bye! See you!
HEY, ARE YOU OKAY?

I'M FINE.
REALLY.
YEAH. BECAUSE YOU LOOK SO FINE.
YOU'D TELL ME IF THERE WAS SOMETHING GOING ON...RIGHT?
O-OF COURSE...

WHAT ARE THOSE
TWO UP TO?

WHY IS MORGAN SO INTENT ON MAKING ME QUIT THE HOMECOMING QUEEN RACE?
SHE CAN'T POSSIBLY THINK I HAVE A CHANCE OF WINNING...OR THAT SHE DOES...
...NOT WITH JENNIFER IN THE RUNNING.
JENNIFER'S THE QUEEN...NOT ME. AND DEFINITELY NOT MORGAN. NOT IN THIS LIFE...
...AND NOT IN HER LAST LIFE, EITHER...

WAIT... DID I REALLY JUST THINK THAT?!

HEY...
ARE YOU SURE YOU'RE ALL RIGHT?
OH...YEAH. SORRY. I'M FINE.

OKAY.
SO... TOMORROW NIGHT'S THE NIGHT, THEN?

TOMORROW NIGHT?

THE BIG DINNER?
MY PARENTS?
YOUR PARENTS?
THE BIG FUN GET-TOGETHER?

RIGHT!
TOMORROW NIGHT!

YOU HAVEN'T CHANGED YOUR MIND, HAVE YOU?
WANT TO CANCEL? BECAUSE THAT'D BE FINE WITH--
NO!
TOMORROW NIGHT! SEVEN SHARP!
SEVEN SHARP.
CHU

BRRRRRRRING
See ya!

TOMORROW NIGHT... IT HAS TO GO WELL TOMORROW NIGHT. IT JUST HAS TO!

# CHAPTER SIX

CHATTER
CHATTER
CHATTER

THEY'RE LATE.
THEY'LL BE HERE.

THEY AREN'T COMING.

OH, WILL, OF COURSE THEY'RE COMING.
LET'S NOT BE PESSIMISTIC.

I HAVE AN IDEA. LET'S JUST GO HOME.
SLAM
NO!
WE CAN'T!!

ELLIE...
MURMUR
MURMUR
MURMUR
MURMUR

SORRY.
I MEAN, NO. WE CAN'T.
WE HAVE THIS NICE TABLE. WE MIGHT AS WELL ORDER.

THE CRAB CAKES LOOK GOOD.
MENU

ELLIE, LOOK, YOU TRIED. I APPRECIATE IT. I REALLY DO.
BUT IT'S NO USE. MY DAD HATES ME. WE'VE GOT TO FACE THE FACT THAT HE'S NOT--

ADMIRAL WAGNER!
YOU CAME!

I'M SO SORRY WE'RE LATE...
WILL, IT'S SO GOOD TO SEE YOU.
IT'S BEEN TOO LONG.
HI, MOM.
YOU, TOO.

SON.
DAD.
GRIP

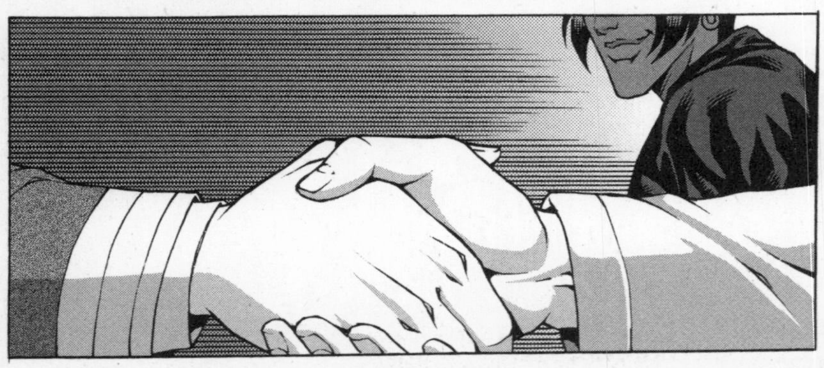

UH...I'M NOT SURE WHAT, EXACTLY--
I'M SO SORRY.
I KNOW WHAT A SHOCK THIS MUST BE TO ALL OF YOU--ESPECIALLY YOU, WILL, AND ELLIE.

BUT PLEASE ALLOW US TO ASSURE YOU THAT MARCO WOULDN'T HAVE BEEN RELEASED FROM THE HOSPITAL AND INTO OUR CARE IF HE WASN'T DOING MUCH, MUCH BETTER.
AND HE COULDN'T BE MORE SORRY FOR WHAT HAPPENED ON THAT TERRIBLE DAY IN THE PARK.

THAT'S RIGHT.
I JUST WANT US TO BE A FAMILY AGAIN.
HE REALLY DOES, WILL.
HE BEGGED US TO LET HIM COME ALONG TONIGHT. I REALLY DO HOPE IT'S ALL RIGHT.
IT IS ALL RIGHT, ISN'T IT?
Please?

I DON'T CARE.
LET'S JUST ORDER.

GREAT.
I'LL JUST GET THEM TO SET AN EXTRA PLACE.

CLATTER
CLINK
CLINK

HOW COULD THEY?
HOW COULD THEY HAVE BROUGHT MARCO?

...JUST LIKE ALWAYS.

SO, MARCO.
WHAT ARE YOU GOING TO DO NOW THAT YOU'RE, UH...

YOU CAN SAY IT.
OUT OF THE LOONY BIN.
IF YOU WANT TO PUT IT THAT WAY?

WELL, I'M TAKING COURSES OVER AT THE COMMUNITY COLLEGE, AND VOLUNTEERING AT THE LOCAL REST HOME.
ONCE I GET ENOUGH CREDITS AND REFERENCES, DAD'S GOING TO PUT IN A GOOD WORD FOR ME OVER AT THE ACADEMY--
THBBBT!

IS THERE A PROBLEM, WILL?

NOPE.
NO PROBLEM. SORRY, EVERYBODY.

WE'RE VERY PLEASED WITH THE PROGRESS MARCO HAS BEEN MAKING. HIS DEDICATION AND COMMITMENT SHOW REMARKABLE GROWTH.
AND IT'S NOT TOO LATE FOR YOU, WILL, TO JOIN HIM--
THAT'S OKAY, DAD. THE MILITARY REALLY ISN'T MY THING.
AND JUST WHAT *IS* YOUR *THING?*
SLAM
YOU KNOW, MR. MORTON, WILL'S WORLD CIVILIZATION TEACHER, THINKS WILL IS ONE OF THE BEST--

THAT CRAZY OLD MAN!
THE ONE WHO THINKS WILL IS THE REINCARNATION OF SOME KING?
WHY, I OUGHT TO HAVE NOTIFIED THE SCHOOL BOARD ABOUT THAT OLD QUACK MONTHS AGO!
MR. MORTON'S NOT AN OLD QUACK! HE'S--
I DON'T THINK THIS IS NECESSARILY THE BEST TIME TO TALK ABOUT THIS.
AND WHEN WOULD BE THE BEST TIME?
YOU'RE A SENIOR, WILL. YOU'RE GOING TO HAVE TO DECIDE WHAT YOU'RE GOING TO DO WITH YOUR LIFE SOON, YOU KNOW!

I KNOW WHAT I WANT TO DO WITH MY LIFE, DAD. I WANT TO GO INTO POLITICAL SCIENCE TO LEARN HOW TO HELP PEOPLE.
WHAT I *DON'T* WANT TO DO IS GO TO MILITARY SCHOOL TO LEARN HOW TO KILL PEOPLE.

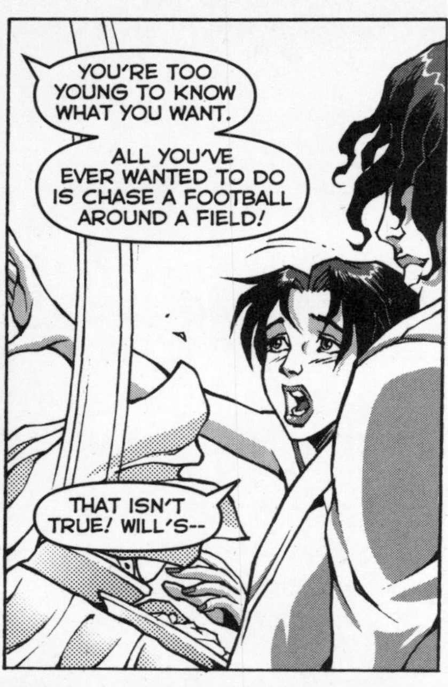
YOU'RE TOO YOUNG TO KNOW WHAT YOU WANT.
ALL YOU'VE EVER WANTED TO DO IS CHASE A FOOTBALL AROUND A FIELD!
THAT ISN'T TRUE! WILL'S--

HOW WOULD YOU EVEN KNOW?
IT'S NOT LIKE YOU'VE EVER BEEN TO EVEN ONE OF MY GAMES.

I'M SORRY IF I HAVE SLIGHTLY MORE IMPORTANT THINGS TO DO THAN GO TO HIGH SCHOOL FOOTBALL GAMES.

JUST LIKE I HAVE SLIGHTLY MORE IMPORTANT THINGS TO DO THAN SIT HERE AND LISTEN TO THIS INSANITY.

I-I'M SORRY.

ARE WE READY TO LOOK AT THE DESSERT MENU?

NO...?
MAYBE...I'LL COME BACK LATER.

DUDE. THINK ABOUT WHAT YOU'RE DOING.
ARE YOU REALLY GOING TO THROW AWAY YOUR TICKET TO ONE OF THE BEST SCHOOLS IN THE COUNTRY BECAUSE SOME NUTTY OLD TEACHER TOLD YOU THAT YOU'RE A REINCARNATED *KING?*
I MEAN, YEAH, I BELIEVED IT FOR A WHILE TOO...BUT I WAS *CRAZY,* REMEMBER?

I DON'T BELIEVE I'M A REINCARNATED KING, MARCO.
WHAT I DO BELIEVE IS THAT I GOT SHORT-CHANGED IN THE PATERNAL DEPARTMENT. *FRATERNAL*, TOO.
THAT'S COLD, BRO. REALLY COLD.
ALL I'M TRYING TO DO IS HELP.
SNATCH
YEAH? WELL, THE BEST WAY YOU CAN HELP IS BY STAYING AWAY FROM ME...AND MY GIRL!

MURMUR
MURMUR

CHECK, PLEASE!

OKAY. THAT DIDN'T GO VERY WELL.
INSTEAD OF BRINGING WILL CLOSER TOGETHER WITH HIS DAD, ALL I DID WAS DRIVE THEM FARTHER APART. AND WILL STILL DOESN'T BELIEVE HE'S KING ARTHUR, REINCARNATED.

NOT THAT I BELIEVE IT, EITHER, NECESSARILY... EXCEPT...EXCEPT...WHAT IF IT IS TRUE?
I MEAN...ALL THOSE NIGHTMARES HAVE TO MEAN SOMETHING, RIGHT? WHAT IF MR. MORTON IS RIGHT, AND THE MERLIN PROPHECY IS REAL? I'VE JUST GOT TO TELL HIM...

KNOCK
KNOCK

COME IN.

HI...

HEY.
WHAT IS IT? IT'S A LITTLE EARLY FOR NIGHTMARES ALREADY, ISN'T IT?

THAT'S WHAT I WANTED TO TALK TO YOU ABOUT... YOU ASKED ME TODAY IF SOMETHING WAS GOING ON...
I KNEW IT.
WHAT IS THIS ABOUT? HOMECOMING QUEEN? MY DAD? OR...MARCO?

I WISH IT WERE THAT SIMPLE.
WILL...IT'S ABOUT SOMETHING MR. MORTON TOLD ME THE OTHER DAY.
MR. MORTON?
WHY?
WHAT DID HE SAY?

WILL, I KNOW WE LAUGH ABOUT, YOU KNOW, THE KING ARTHUR THING. BUT THIS TIME, SOMETHING MR. MORTON SAID...
...AND THE FACT THAT I KEEP HAVING THESE NIGHTMARES... AND MARCO COMING BACK...AND THE THING WITH YOUR DAD.... AND HOMECOMING--ALL AT THE SAME TIME...
I'M KIND OF STARTING TO BELIEVE IT. IT'S ALL COMING TOGETHER IN THIS CREEPY WAY.

WHAT IS?
ELLE, YOU'RE NOT MAKING ANY SENSE.
IT'S JUST THAT MR. MORTON SAYS THAT ACCORDING TO AN ANCIENT PROPHECY, IN ORDER FOR THE PLANET TO ACHIEVE TRUE PEACE, THE REINCARNATION OF ARTHUR--UM, THAT'D BE YOU--MUST BELIEVE HE IS TRULY A KING.
AND IF THIS DOESN'T HAPPEN BY THE HUNTER'S MOON--WHICH IS TOMORROW NIGHT--ETERNAL PEACE WILL NEVER HAPPEN!

ELLE!
HA
HA
HA!
WILL!
IT'S NOT FUNNY!

WHAT ARE YOU TALKING ABOUT?
IT'S FREAKING HILARIOUS!
Chuckle
Chuckle

NO, IT'S NOT!
WILL, IF YOU DON'T BELIEVE--TRULY BELIEVE--THAT YOU'RE THE REINCARNATION OF KING ARTHUR BY HOMECOMING TOMORROW NIGHT, SOMETHING TERRIBLE WILL HAPPEN!

LIKE WHAT?
THE WORLD IS GOING TO END?

YES!

WILL--MR. MORTON WAS RIGHT BEFORE. REMEMBER WHAT HAPPENED WITH MARCO?
AND NOW... HE'S BACK. MARCO'S *BACK.*
ELLE. IS *THAT* WHY YOU'RE SO WORRIED ALL THE TIME?
IS *THAT* WHY YOU KEEP HAVING THOSE NIGHTMARES?

PLEASE, WILL... JUST PROMISE ME.
PROMISE ME YOU'LL TRY TO BELIEVE.
ELLE, YOU KNOW I'D NEVER LET ANYTHING HAPPEN TO YOU. MARCO WOULDN'T DARE LAY A FINGER ON YOU WHILE I'M AROUND...
IT'S NOT ME I'M WORRIED ABOUT.

Mmngh...

TIG?
Meow...

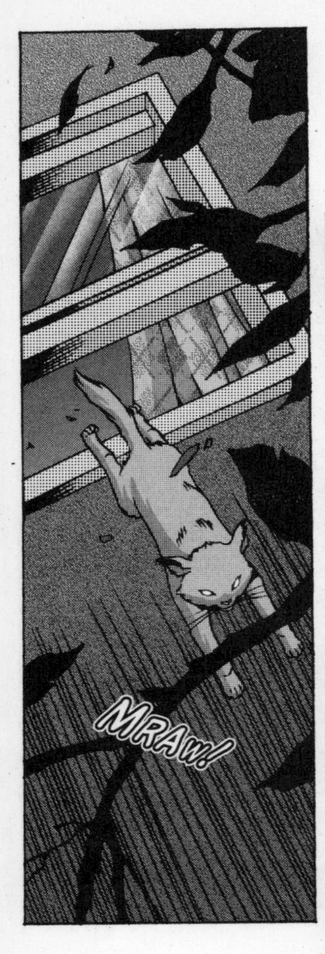
MRAW!

TMP
TMP
TMP

TIG?
HOW DID YOU GET OUTSIDE?

HERE, KITTY...
WHOOOOSH

TIG? WHERE ARE YOU?!

WHOOOOOSH

Y-YOU!
HELLO, ELLIE.
TO BE CONTINUED...

In the Next

# Avalon High
## Coronation

Volume 3: Hunter's Moon

Will's got to win the Homecoming game . . . or it's game over . . . for Planet Earth.

For all the books about Mia and more by

# MEG CABOT

check out the following pages!

You'll find:

- Details about King Arthur and his court
- A sneak peek of *Jinx*, one of Meg's novels!
- Blurbs about Meg's other exciting books
- Info about the Princess Diaries series

Still not enough?
For even more about Meg Cabot, go to:

**www.harperteen.com/megcabot**

You can read Meg's online diary,
find the latest info on her books,
take quizzes, and get advice
on how to handle the paparazzi.

## Who was the real King Arthur?

*"The Pendragons were way dysfunctional as far as families go. Jerry Springer would have* loved *them."*
*—Ellie Harrison,* Avalon High

In *Avalon High*, Ellie Harrison discovers that she—along with her crush, Will, his best friend, Lance, and his not-so-steady girlfriend, Jennifer—are just like the characters in the legend of King Arthur. In fact, they may even *be* the kings and queens of the past—reborn and living in modern-day America.

But just who was the real King Arthur—and the rest of his crew at Camelot? Their identities are entwined with myths and stories, but historians have discovered some truth behind the legends. Here's a look at some of their discoveries.

### King Arthur: A Uniter, Not a Divider

The real King Arthur lived around the year 500, when horrible wars and invading barbarians left England in shambles. Around this time, a strong king emerged and fought back the Saxons, Britain's biggest threat in the North, bringing peace and prosperity to the land for about forty years.

The real Arthur would not have had knights in shining armor, tournaments, or even stone castles in his day. His armor would have been made of chain mail and leather, and his castles would have been built with dirt and stones. Many of the embellishments that we know (like the tournaments and even the Round Table) were added by later writers. The most famous of these are Geoffrey of Monmouth, a cleric in the 1100s, and Sir Thomas Malory, a former knight turned writer for the king, in the 1400s.

### Guinevere: Queen of Hearts

Guinevere's identity is even more mysterious than Arthur's. Some historians believe she was a queen before Arthur married her—which explains her fierce independence. In fact, Arthur might have married her to gain land or form a political alliance. The legends agree that Guinevere was the most beautiful woman in the world. Some describe her as slender, with fair skin, dark hair, and a wreath of gold leaves around her head.

Guinevere was unfaithful to Arthur but not disloyal. She respected him, though she did not love him. She often ran his court in his absence. After he died, she became a nun.

### Lancelot: Medieval Hottie

Lancelot first makes his appearance in a poem by Chrétien de Troyes, a twelfth-century poet hired by a noblewoman, Marie de Champagne. (Marie was the daughter of a woman who eventually married King Henry II.) Chrétien was influenced by Scottish legends, but mainly wrote to appeal to the ladies of the court. So he added lots of romance to Lancelot's adventures.

According to Chrétien's stories, Lancelot was raised by the Lady of the Lake, the same spirit who gave Arthur the sword Excalibur. Lancelot was the handsomest of Arthur's knights, and the most loyal. He was daring, strong, and even had his own kingdom in France. Of course, women loved him.

King Arthur knighted Lancelot, but Queen Guinevere presented him with his sword. By the rules of chivalry, Lancelot was then considered her knightly servant and defender. But soon Lancelot realized his love of Guinevere was beyond that of courtly love—and after saving her from a kidnapping, the two began a secret affair.

### Mordred: Britain's Bad Boy

In some legends, Mordred was Arthur's son. (His mother was Arthur's half sister, Morgause.) In others, he was Arthur's half brother. But all versions agree: Mordred was a villain. Jealous of Arthur's success, Mordred wanted to take over the kingdom. He plotted with other knights to expose Guinevere and Lancelot's affair. When Arthur didn't believe the charges, Mordred gathered the other knights outside of Guinevere's bedchamber. Lancelot, who was, of course, inside with Guinevere, escaped by killing all of the knights but Mordred. Arthur vowed to find him, and soon Arthur and Lancelot's armies were embroiled in a terrible war. While his men fought, Arthur was toppled at home by the scheming Mordred.

### Merlin: Wizard, Guidance Counselor

According to the legends, Merlin was a magician as well as an important advisor to Arthur and Arthur's father, Uther Pendragon. Merlin saved Arthur's life many times. He also helped Arthur draw the sword from the stone as a young boy, proving him to be the future king. Though Arthur didn't heed the warning, Merlin revealed that Arthur's end would be marked by tragedy.

### The Lady of the Lake: Mystery Woman

Some historians believe the Lady of the Lake was a position, similar to president or team captain, which was occupied by several different women in different legends. One Lady walked on water, another was a mermaid who raised Lancelot, and yet another was an apprentice to Merlin.

In one story by Sir Thomas Malory, Arthur forged a special relationship with the Lady of the Lake. After losing one of his early battles, Arthur asked Merlin for a new weapon. Merlin, as mysterious as ever, brought him to the edge of a lake. As Arthur looked into the crystal-clear water, an arm appeared with a sword in its hand. The sword then disappeared, leaving a beautiful lady in its place. Arthur asked her if he could have the sword. The Lady of the Lake answered that he could, but that Arthur would have to give her a gift if asked. Arthur agreed, and the sword became Excalibur, with which he won the most famous battles of the Dark Ages.

### Elaine of Astolat: Heartbroken Chick

Elaine was a noble lady who fell wildly in love with Lancelot. When her love was not returned, she didn't eat or sleep for ten days. After her death, her richly dressed body was sent down the river on a barge to Westminster, where King Arthur found it. She held a note in her hands for Lancelot.

Elaine is considered the embodiment of unrequited love. Alfred Lord Tennyson, a poet in the nineteenth century, wrote about her in his famous poem, *The Lady of Shalott*.

## *Want to learn more?*

**There are many books about Camelot. Here are just a few:**

**Nonfiction**

*Women of Camelot* by Mary Hoffman
*King Arthur and His Knights of the Round Table* by Roger Lancelyn Green
*Le Morte D'Arthur* by Sir Thomas Malory
*King Arthur* by Norma Lorre Goodrich
*The History of the Kings of Britain* by Geoffrey of Monmouth

**Fiction**

*The Crystal Cave* by Mary Stewart
*The Hollow Hills* by Mary Stewart
*The Last Enchantment* by Mary Stewart
*The Wicked Day* by Mary Stewart
*The Mists of Avalon* by Marion Zimmer Bradley
*Black Horses for the King* by Anne McCaffrey
*The Once and Future King* by T. H. White

Is it just bad luck . . .
Or could it be witchcraft?

# CHAPTER ONE

The thing is, my luck's always been rotten. Just look at my name: Jean. Not Jean Marie, or Jeanine, or Jeanette, or even Jeanne. Just Jean. Did you know in France, they name *boys* Jean? It's French for John.

And okay, I don't live in France. But still. I'm basically a girl named John. If I lived in France, anyway.

This is the kind of luck I have. The kind of luck I've had since before Mom even filled out my birth certificate.

So it wasn't any big surprise to me when the cab driver didn't help me with my suitcase. I'd already had to endure arriving at the airport to find no one there to greet me, and then got no answer to my many phone calls, asking where my aunt and uncle were. Did they not want me after all? Had they changed their minds? Had they heard about my bad luck—all the way from Iowa—and decided they didn't want any of it to rub off on them?

But even if that were true—and as I'd told myself a million times since arriving at baggage claim, where they were supposed to have met me, and seeing no one but skycaps and limo drivers with little signs with everyone's names on them but mine—there was nothing I could do about it. I certainly couldn't go home. It was New York City—and Aunt Evelyn and Uncle Ted's house—or bust.

So when the cab driver, instead of getting out and helping me with my bags, just pushed a little button so that the trunk popped open a few inches, it wasn't the worst thing that had ever happened to me. It wasn't even the worst thing that had happened to me that *day.*

I pulled out my bags, each of which had to weigh fifty thousand pounds, at least—except my violin case, of course—and then closed the trunk again, all while standing in the middle of East Sixty-ninth Street, with a line of cars behind me, honking impatiently because they couldn't pass, due to the fact that there was a Stanley Steemer van double-parked across the street from my aunt and uncle's building.

Why me? Really. I'd like to know.

The cab pulled away so fast, I practically had to leap between two parked cars to keep from getting run over. The honking stopped as the line of cars that had been waiting behind the cab started moving again, their drivers all throwing me dirty looks as they went by.

It was all the dirty looks that did it—made me realize I was really in New York City. At last.

And yeah, I'd seen the skyline from the cab as it crossed the Triboro Bridge . . . the island of Manhattan, in all its gritty glory, with the Empire State Building sticking up from the middle of it like a big glittery middle finger.

But the dirty looks were what really cinched it. No one back in Hancock would ever have been that mean to someone who was clearly from out of town.

Not that all that many people visit Hancock. But whatever.

Then there was the street I was standing on. It was one of those streets that look exactly like the ones they always show on TV when they're trying to let you know something is set in New York. Like on *Law and Order*. You know, the narrow three- or four-story brownstones with the brightly painted front doors and the stone stoops. . . .

According to my mom, most brownstones in New York City were originally single-family homes when they were built way back in the 1800s. But now they've been divided up into apartments, so that there's one—or sometimes even two or more families—per floor.

Not Mom's sister Evelyn's brownstone, though. Aunt Evelyn and Uncle Ted Gardiner own all four floors of their brownstone. That's practically one floor per person, since Aunt Evelyn and Uncle Ted only have three kids, my cousins Tory, Teddy, and Alice.

Back home, we just have two floors, but there are seven people living on them. And only one bathroom.

Not that I'm complaining. Still, ever since my sister Courtney discovered blow-outs, it's been pretty grim at home.

But as tall as my aunt and uncle's house was, it was really narrow—just three windows across. Still, it was a very pretty townhouse, painted gray, with lighter gray trim. The door was a bright, cheerful yellow. There were yellow flower boxes along the base of each window, flower boxes from which bright red—and obviously newly planted, since it was only the middle of April, and not quite warm enough for them—geraniums spilled.

It was nice to know that, even in a sophisticated city like New York, people still realized how homey and welcoming a box of geraniums could be. The sight of those geraniums cheered me up a little.

Like maybe Aunt Evelyn and Uncle Ted just forgot I was arriving today, and hadn't deliberately failed to meet me at the airport because they'd changed their minds about letting me come to stay.

Like everything was going to be all right, after all.

Yeah. With my luck, probably not.

I started up the steps to the front door of 326 East Sixty-ninth Street, then realized I couldn't make it with both bags and my violin. Leaving one bag on the sidewalk, I dragged the other up the steps with me, my violin tucked under one arm. I deposited the first suitcase and my violin case at the top of the steps, then hurried back down for the second suitcase, which I'd left on the sidewalk.

Only I guess I took the steps a little too fast, since I

nearly tripped and fell flat on my face on the sidewalk. I managed to catch myself at the last moment by grabbing some of the wrought-iron fencing the Gardiners had put up around their trash cans. As I hung there, a little stunned from my near catastrophe, a stylishly dressed old lady walking what appeared to be a rat on a leash (only it must have been a dog, since it was wearing a tartan coat) passed by and shook her head at me. Like I'd taken a nosedive down the Gardiners' front steps on purpose to startle her, or something.

Back in Hancock, if a person had seen someone else almost fall down the stairs—even someone like me, who nearly falls down the stairs every single day—they would have said something like, "Are you all right?"

In Manhattan, however, things were clearly different.

It wasn't until the old lady and her pet rat passed all the way by that I heard a click. Straightening—and finding that my hands were covered in rust from where I'd gripped the fence—I saw that the door to 326 East Sixty-ninth Street had opened, and that a young, pretty, blond girl was peering down at me from the top of the stoop.

"Hello?" she said curiously.

I forgot about the old lady and her rat and my near-pavement-dive. I smiled and hurried back up the steps. Even though I couldn't quite believe how much she'd changed, I was so glad to see her—

—and was so worried she wasn't going to feel the same way about seeing me.

"Hi," I said. "Hi, Tory."

The young woman, very petite and very blond, blinked at me without recognition.

"No," she said. "No, I am not Tory. I am Petra." For the first time, I noticed that the girl had an accent . . . a European one. "I am the Gardiners' au pair."

"Oh," I said uncertainly. No one had said anything to me about an au pair. Fortunately, I knew what one was, because of an episode of *Law and Order* I saw once, where the au pair was suspected of killing the kid she was supposed to be watching.

I stretched my rust-stained right hand out toward Petra. "Hi," I said. "I'm Jean Honeychurch. Evelyn Gardiner is my aunt. . . ."

"Jean?" Petra had reached out and automatically taken my hand. Now her grasp on it tightened. "Oh, you mean Jinx?"

I winced, and not just at the girl's hard grip—she was really strong for someone so little.

No, I winced because my reputation had so clearly preceded me, if the au pair knew me as Jinx instead of Jean.

"Right," I said. Because what else could I do? So much for getting a fresh new start in a place where no one knew me by my less-than-flattering nickname. "My family calls me Jinx."

And would continue to do so forever, if I couldn't turn my luck around.

"But you are not supposed to arrive until tomorrow!" Petra cried.

The tight ball of worry in my stomach loosened. Just a little.

I should have known. I should have known Aunt Evelyn wouldn't have completely forgotten about me.

"No," I said. "Today. I'm supposed to arrive today."

"Oh, no," Petra said, still shaking my hand up and down. My fingers were losing all circulation. Also, the places I'd skinned grabbing the wrought-iron fence weren't feeling too good, either. "I'm sure your aunt and uncle said tomorrow. Oh! They will be so upset! They were going to meet you at the airport. Alice even made a sign. . . . Did you come all this way by yourself? In a taxi? I am so sorry for you! Oh, my goodness, come in, come in!"

With a heartiness that belied her delicate frame—but

matched her handshake—Petra insisted on grabbing both of my bags, leaving my violin to me, and carrying them inside herself. Their extreme heaviness didn't seem to bother her at all, and it only took me a couple of minutes to find out why, Petra being almost as big a talker as my best friend, Stacy, back home: Petra had moved from her native Germany to the United States because she's studying to be a physical therapist.

In fact, she told me she goes to physical therapy school every morning in Westchester, which is a suburb just outside of New York City, where, when she's not in class, she has to lift heavy people and help them into spas, then teach them to use their arms and stuff again, after an accident or stroke.

Which explained why she was so strong. Because of the lifting of heavy patients, and all.

Petra was living with the Gardiners, paying for her room and board by caring for my younger cousins. Then, while the kids were in school every day, she went to Westchester to learn more physical therapy stuff. In another year, she'll have her license and can get a job in a rehabilitation center.

"The Gardiners have been *so* kind to me," Petra said, carrying my suitcases to a third-floor guest room as if they didn't weigh more than a couple of CDs.

It didn't even seem like it was necessary for Petra to take a breath between sentences. Amazingly, English was not even her first language.

Which meant she could probably speak faster in her native tongue.

"They even pay me three hundred dollars a week," Petra went on. "Imagine, living in Manhattan rent-free, with all of your food paid for as well, and someone giving you three hundred dollars a week! My friends back home in Bonn say it is too good to be true. Mr. and Mrs. Gardiner are like a mother and father to me now. And I love Teddy and Alice like they are my own children. Well, I am only twenty, and Teddy is ten, so I guess he could not be my son. But my own little brother, maybe. Here, now. Here is your room."

My room? I peered around the doorframe. Judging by the glimpses I'd had of the rest of the house on our way up the stairs, I knew I was going to be living in the lap of luxury for the next few months. . . .

But the room in which Petra set my bags down took my breath away. It was totally beautiful . . . white-walled with cream-and-gilt furniture, and pink silk drapes. There was a marble fireplace on one side—"It does not work, this one," Petra informed me sadly, like I had been counting on a working fireplace in my new bedroom, or something—and a private bathroom on the other. Sunlight filtered through the windows, making a dappled pattern on the light pink carpeting.

Of course, I knew right away something was wrong. This was the nicest bedroom I'd ever seen. It was a hundred times nicer than my bedroom back home. And I'd had to share that bedroom with Courtney and Sarabeth, my two younger sisters. This would, in fact, be my first time sleeping in a room of my own.

EVER.

And never in my life had I so much as entertained the idea of having my own bathroom.

This was just not possible.

But I could tell from the casual way Petra was going around, flicking imaginary dust off things, that it *was* possible. Not just possible, but . . . the way things were.

"Wow," was all I could say. It was the first word I'd been able to get in since Petra had begun speaking, down at the front door.

"Yes," Petra said. She thought I meant the room. But really, I'd meant . . . well, *everything*. "It is very nice, yes? I have my own apartment in this house, with a private entrance—downstairs, you know? The ground floor. You probably did not see it. The door is underneath the stoop to the townhouse. There is also a back door to the garden. It is a little private apartment. I have my own kitchen, too. The children come down at night sometimes, and I help them with their homework, and sometimes we watch the TV together, all snug. It is very nice."

"You're not kidding," I breathed. Mom had told me that Aunt Evelyn and her family were doing well—her husband, my uncle Ted, had recently gotten a promotion to president of whatever company it was he worked for, while Evelyn, an interior decorator, had added a couple of supermodels to her client list.

Still, nothing could have prepared me for . . . this.

And it was mine. All mine.

Well, for the time being, anyway. Until I messed it up, somehow.

And, me being me, I knew that wouldn't take long. But I could still enjoy it while it lasted.

"Mr. and Mrs. Gardiner will be so sorry they were not home to greet you," Petra was saying as she went to the side of the king-sized bed and began fastidiously fluffing the half-dozen pillows beneath the tufted headboard. "And they'll be even sadder that they got the days mixed up. They are both still at work. Teddy and Alice will be home from school soon, though. They are both very excited their cousin Jinx is coming to stay. Alice has made you a sign to welcome you. She was going to hold it at the airport when they greeted you, but now . . . well, perhaps you could hang it on the wall here in your room? You must pretend to be pleased by it, even if you are not, because she worked very hard on it. Mrs. Gardiner did not put anything on your walls, you see, because she wanted to wait to see what you are like. She says it has been five years since they last saw you!"

Petra looked at me in wonder. Apparently, families in Germany lived a lot closer and visited one another a lot more often than families in the U.S. . . . or *my* family, anyway.

I nodded. "Yes, that sounds about right. Aunt Evelyn and Uncle Ted last came to visit when I was eleven. . . ." My voice trailed off. That's because I'd just noticed that in the massive bathroom, the fixtures were all brass and shaped like swan necks, with the water coming out of the bird's carved beak. Even the towel bar had swan wings on the ends. My mouth was starting to feel a little dry at the sight of all this luxury. I mean, what had I ever done to deserve all this?

Nothing. Especially lately.

Which was actually why I was in New York.

*Ellie has a hunch that nothing is as it seems in*

# AVALON HIGH

Avalon High seems like a typical school, with typical students. There's Lance, the jock. Jennifer, the cheerleader. And Will, senior class president, quarterback, and all-around good guy. But not everyone at Avalon High is who they appear to be . . . not even, as new student Ellie is about to discover, herself. What part does she play in the drama that is unfolding? What if the chain of coincidences she has pieced together means—like the court of King Arthur—tragedy is fast approaching Avalon High? Worst of all, what if there's nothing she can do about it?

*A hilarious new novel about getting in trouble, getting caught, and getting the guy!*

Katie Ellison has everything going for her senior year—a great job, two boyfriends, and a good shot at being crowned Quahog Princess of her small coastal town in Connecticut. So why does Tommy Sullivan have to come back into her life? Sure, they used to be friends, but that was before the huge screwup that turned their whole town against him. Now he's back, and making Katie's perfect life a total disaster. Can the Quahog Princess and the *freak* have anything in common? Could they even be falling for each other?

www.harperteen.com

# the mediator

Suze can see ghosts. Which is kind of a pain most of the time, but when Suze moves to California and finds Jesse, the ghost of a nineteenth-century hottie haunting her bedroom, things begin to look up.

THE MEDIATOR 1:

*Shadowland*

THE MEDIATOR 2:

*Ninth Key*

THE MEDIATOR 3:

*Reunion*

THE MEDIATOR 4:

*Darkest Hour*

THE MEDIATOR 5:

*Haunted*

THE MEDIATOR 6:

*Twilight*

## ALL-AMERICAN *Girl*

What if you were going about your average life when all of a sudden, you accidentally saved the president's life? Oops! This is exactly what happens to Samantha Madison while she's busy eating cookies and rummaging through CDs. Suddenly her life as a sophomore in high school, usually spent pining after her older sister's boyfriend or living in the academic shadows of her younger sister's genius, is sent spinning. Now everyone at school—and in the country!—seems to think Sam is some kind of hero. Everyone, that is, except herself. But the number-one reason Samantha Madison's life has gone completely insane is that, on top of all this . . . the president's son just might be in love with her!

## *Ready* OR *Not*

In this sequel to *All-American Girl*, everyone thinks Samantha Madison—who, yes, DID save the president's life—is ready: Her parents think she's ready to learn the value of a dollar by working part-time, her art teacher thinks she's ready for "life drawing" (who knew that would mean "naked people"?!), the president thinks she's ready to make a speech on live TV, and her boyfriend (who just happens to be David, the president's son) seems to think they're ready to take their relationship to the Next Level. . . .

The only person who's not sure Samantha Madison is ready for any of the above is Samantha herself!

READ ALL OF THE BOOKS ABOUT MIA!

*The Princess Diaries*

THE PRINCESS DIARIES, VOLUME II:
*Princess in the Spotlight*

THE PRINCESS DIARIES, VOLUME III:
*Princess in Love*

THE PRINCESS DIARIES, VOLUME IV:
*Princess in Waiting*

*Valentine Princess*
A PRINCESS DIARIES BOOK (VOLUME IV AND A QUARTER)

THE PRINCESS DIARIES, VOLUME IV AND A HALF:
*Project Princess*

THE PRINCESS DIARIES, VOLUME V:
*Princess in Pink*

THE PRINCESS DIARIES, VOLUME VI:
*Princess in Training*

*The Princess Present:*
A PRINCESS DIARIES BOOK (VOLUME VI AND A HALF)

THE PRINCESS DIARIES, VOLUME VII:
*Party Princess*

*Sweet Sixteen Princess:*
A PRINCESS DIARIES BOOK (VOLUME VII AND A HALF)

THE PRINCESS DIARIES, VOLUME VIII:
*Princess on the Brink*

ILLUSTRATED BY CHESLEY MCLAREN

*Princess Lessons:*
A PRINCESS DIARIES BOOK

*Perfect Princess:*
A PRINCESS DIARIES BOOK

*Holiday Princess:*
A PRINCESS DIARIES BOOK

*Girl-next-door Jenny Greenley goes stir-crazy (or star-crazy?) in Meg Cabot's*

## TEEN IDOL

Jenny Greenley's good at solving problems—so good she's the school paper's anonymous advice columnist. But when nineteen-year-old screen sensation Luke Striker comes to Jenny's small town to research a role, he creates havoc that even level-headed Jenny isn't sure she can repair . . . especially since she's right in the middle of all of it. Can Jenny, who always manages to be there for everybody else, learn to take her own advice, and find true love at last?

*Does Steph have what it takes?*

## HOW TO BE Popular

Everyone wants to be popular—or at least, Stephanie Landry does. Steph's been the least popular girl in her class since a certain cherry Super Big Gulp catastrophe five years earlier. And she's determined to get in with the It Crowd this year—no matter what! After all, Steph's got a secret weapon: an old book called—what else?—*How to Be Popular*.

Turns out . . . it's easy to become popular. What isn't so easy? Staying that way!

*But wait!*
*There's more by Meg:*

NICOLA AND THE VISCOUNT
VICTORIA AND THE ROGUE

THE BOY NEXT DOOR
BOY MEETS GIRL
EVERY BOY'S GOT ONE
QUEEN OF BABBLE
QUEEN OF BABBLE IN THE BIG CITY
SIZE 12 IS NOT FAT
SIZE 14 IS NOT FAT EITHER

# ABOUT THE ILLUSTRATOR

*JINKY CORONADO*

WINNER OF A DOZEN BEAUTY PAGEANTS IN HER NATIVE PHILIPPINES AS WELL AS A FORMER MISS POND'S ASIA, JINKY CORONADO GRADUATED WITH A DEGREE IN MARKETING AND A MINOR IN ART FROM THE UNIVERSITY OF SAN AUGUSTIN IN ILOILO, PHILIPPINES. HER FIRST CLAIM TO FAME IN THE USA WAS WRITING, DRAWING, AND STARRING AS THE COVER MODEL AND MAIN CHARACTER FOR BANZAI GIRL AND ITS NOW-BEING-PUBLISHED SEQUEL, BANZAI GIRLS, BOTH FULL-COLOR SERIES DEPICTING HERSELF AS AN ASIAN SCHOOLGIRL BATTLING FILIPINO-STYLE "URBAN LEGENDS" AND WEAVING HER REAL FRIENDS AND FAMILY INTO THE STORY TAPESTRY. A SECOND BANZAI GIRLS GRAPHIC NOVEL WILL BE PUBLISHED SUMMER 2008, WITH A BIG BOOK OF BANZAI SCHEDULED FOR 2009. JINKY AND HER SISTER MICHELLE EVEN RELEASED A MUSIC CD, "BANZAI GIRLS," IN THE PHILIPPINES, AND THEY HAVE BEEN THE SUBJECTS OF THREE CALENDARS. JINKY HAS NOW ILLUSTRATED TWO VOLUMES OF AVALON HIGH AND IS LOOKING FORWARD TO A THIRD.